REPTILES & AMPHIBIANS

Lucy Dowling

New York

Published in 2015 by Windmill Books, An Imprint of Rosen Publishing
29 East 21st Street, New York, NY 10010

Copyright © 2015 by Miles Kelly Publishing Ltd/Windmill Books, An Imprint of Rosen Publishing

All rights reserved. No part of this book may be reproduced in any form without permission in writing from the publisher, except by a reviewer.

US Editor: Joshua Shadowens
Publishing Director: Belinda Gallagher
Creative Director: Jo Cowan
Assistant Editor: Lucy Dowling
Volume Design: Sally Lace
Cover Designer: Jo Cowan
Indexer: Hilary Bird
Production Manager: Elizabeth Collins
Reprographics: Stephan Davis, Thom Allaway, Lorraine King

All artwork from the Miles Kelly Artwork Bank
Cover: Eric Isselee/Shutterstock.com

Library of Congress Cataloging-in-Publication Data

Dowling, Lucy, author.
 Reptiles & amphibians / by Lucy Dowling.
    pages cm. — (Animal Q & A)
 Includes index.
 ISBN 978-1-4777-9194-3 (library binding) — ISBN 978-1-4777-9195-0 (pbk.) — ISBN 978-1-4777-9196-7 (6-pack)
 1. Reptiles—Miscellanea—Juvenile literature. 2. Amphibians—Miscellanea—Juvenile literature. 3. Children's questions and answers. I. Title. II. Title: Reptiles and amphibians.
 QL644.2.D69 2015
 597—dc23
                              2014001239

Manufactured in the United States of America

CPSIA Compliance Information: Batch # WS14WM: For Further Information contact Windmill Books, New York, New York at 1-866-478-0556

Contents

What is a reptile?	4
Why do reptiles sunbathe?	4
What is an amphibian?	5
Why do frogs cross the road?	6
When do amphibians sleep?	7
Can lizards dance?	7
Why do amphibians lay eggs?	8
Where do amphibians grow up?	9
Which toad carries eggs on its back?	9
Where do reptiles lay their eggs?	10
Are reptile eggs strong?	11
Do baby crocodiles cry?	11
Why do lizards stick to walls?	12
Why do chameleons have long tongues?	12
Which reptile can fly?	13
Why do snakes stick out their tongues?	14
Can you see through a gecko?	15
Why can't iguanas blink?	15

Why do snakes squeeze their food?	16
Why do snakes slither?	16
Which snake is a copycat?	17
Are frogs dangerous?	18
Can a lizard's tail fall off?	18
Why do snakes shed their skin?	19
Which lizard can run on two legs?	20
Are toads colourful?	21
Do turtles play tricks?	21
Do reptiles eat amphibians?	22
Glossary	23
Further Reading	23
Index	24
Websites	24

What is a reptile?

Python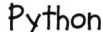

Reptiles are cold-blooded animals. This means that they cannot control their body temperature. A reptile's skin is dry and scaly. There are four kinds of reptile — snakes and lizards, crocodiles, tortoises and turtles and the tuatara, a kind of lizard.

Why do reptiles sunbathe?

Reptiles do a lot of sunbathing! This is called basking, and they do this to get warm so that they can move about. When reptiles are cold they find it difficult to move quickly.

Discover

Next time you are on the beach, bury your legs in the sand to feel how cool it is.

What is an amphibian?

Amphibians are cold-blooded animals. Most amphibians live in or around water. The skin of an amphibian is smooth and wet. The main groups of amphibians are frogs and toads, newts and salamanders and caecilians.

Eastern newt

Head in the sand!

Some amphibians, such as the spadefoot toad, live in very hot places. If it gets too hot, the spadefoot toad buries itself in the sand to cool down!

Cane toad

Why do frogs cross the road?

When spring arrives, amphibians come out of hiding. It is time for them to have their babies. Many amphibians return to the pond or stream where they were born. This may mean a very long journey through towns or over busy roads to breeding grounds.

Frogs

When do amphibians sleep?

When the weather turns cold, amphibians often hide away. They hibernate (go into a deep sleep) under stones and logs. This means that they go to sleep in the autumn, and don't wake up until the next spring!

Mind the frog!

In some places road signs warn drivers that frogs and toads are traveling along the roads to return to their breeding grounds.

Hibernating toad

Can lizards dance?

When the sand gets too hot, the sand lizard of the African Namib Desert performs a strange dance. It lifts its legs up and down off the burning sand or lies on its stomach and raises all its legs at once!

Explore

In the autumn, have a look under some stones and logs for sleeping frogs — try not to wake them!

Why do amphibians lay eggs?

1. Frog spawn

So that their babies can hatch. Amphibians lay eggs in water. Frogs and toads lay a jelly-like string or clump of tiny eggs called spawn. Newts lay one egg at a time. Some amphibians give birth to live young that are born looking like tiny adults.

2. Tadpoles hatch

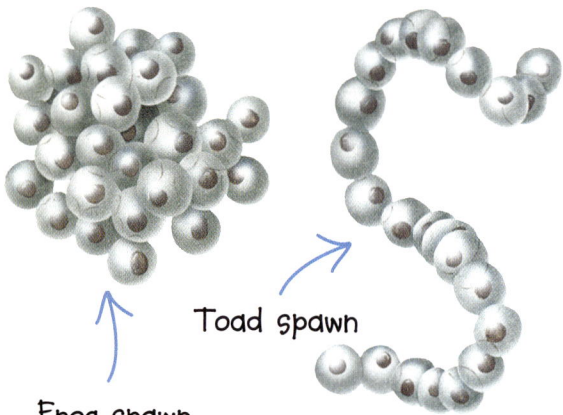

Toad spawn

Frog spawn

Look

In the spring, look carefully in a pond for frog spawn. Check it each day and you might see it hatch into tadpoles!

4. Adult frog

Danger in the air!

Frogs and toads have very good hearing. They also have good senses of taste and smell to check for signs of danger in the air around them.

Where do amphibians grow up?

Most amphibians are born and grow up in fresh water such as ponds, pools, streams and rivers. They move onto dry land when they are adults and return to water to have their babies. This is called breeding. Most amphibians completely change their appearance as they grow.

3. Froglet

Which toad carries eggs on its back?

The female South American Surinam toad carries her eggs on her back. They are put there by her mate. The eggs stay on the mother's back until they hatch.

Where do reptiles lay their eggs?

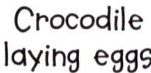

Unlike amphibians, most reptiles lay their eggs on land. The eggs feed and protect the young inside them. The egg yolk provides food for the growing young. The shell protects the baby reptile from the outside world.

Crocodile laying eggs

Good luck!
A mother reptile only looks after her babies for a short time. Then they have to look after themselves. They must learn how to look for food and shelter very quickly.

Snake with eggs

Are reptile eggs strong?

Most reptile eggs are much tougher than those of amphibians. This is because they must survive life out of the water. Lizards and snakes lay eggs with leathery shells. Crocodile and tortoise eggs have a hard shell rather like birds' eggs.

← Nest

Do baby crocodiles cry?

The baby Nile crocodile makes a very high-pitched noise, as if it's crying, when it is ready to hatch. Its mother then helps the baby to hatch by gently rolling the egg in her mouth.

Remember

Can you remember the two ways that an egg helps the young reptile growing inside it?

Why do lizards stick to walls?

Geckos can climb up walls or even walk upside down on ceilings. They are able to cling on because they have five wide-spreading toes, each with sticky toe-pads, on each foot. These strong pads are covered with millions of tiny hairs that grip surfaces tightly.

Why do chameleons have long tongues?

So they can catch their dinner. The chameleon keeps very still. When a tasty fly buzzes past, the chameleon catches it by quickly shooting out its long, sticky tongue and pulling the fly into its mouth.

Chameleon

Pretend
Look in the mirror and stick out your tongue — pretend to be a chameleon catching a fly!

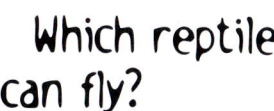
Gecko

Which reptile can fly?

Flying geckos have webbed feet and folds of skin along their legs, tail and sides. This means that they can fly, or glide, over short distances. They do this to either catch food, or to escape from danger.

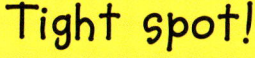

Tight spot!
The chuckwalla lizard gets itself into tight corners. It can jam itself into a crack in a rock, then puff its body up so that enemies cannot pull it out.

Why do snakes stick out their tongues?

Snakes have poor hearing and eyesight. They use their tongue to "smell" the air for food or danger by constantly flicking it in and out. Rattlesnakes can sense heat given off by their prey, even in the dark.

Rattlesnake →

Count
Try to stare at something without blinking. Count how many seconds go by before you need to blink.

Can you see through a gecko?

One African gecko has very thin skin covering its ears. If you were to look at it with its ears lined up, you would be able to see light coming through from the other side of its head!

Strong shell!

A giant tortoise is so big and strong that it can support a 1.1 ton (1 t) weight. This means that it could support a small car!

Iguana

Why can't iguanas blink?

Iguanas have very big eyes and good eyesight, but they cannot blink. Unlike humans, iguanas don't have moveable eyelids. Instead of shutting their eyes to blink, they have special clear eyelids that sweep over their eyes to clean them.

Why do snakes squeeze their food?

Some snakes, like this ratsnake, kill their prey by squeezing it. They wrap their bodies around their meal and squeeze tightly until it stops breathing. Then the snake swallows the prey whole. After a big meal, the snake will not be hungry for a long time.

Why do snakes slither?

Unlike most reptiles, snakes do not have legs to help them move around. Instead they use powerful muscles in their bodies to push and pull themselves forwards. Snakes are also covered in scales, which help them to grip the ground and slither along.

Measure

Using a tape measure, cut a piece of string 23 feet (7 m) long. Lay it down to see how long a reticulated python can be!

Which snake is a copycat?

The milksnake pretends to be the coral snake by copying its colors. This is because the milksnake is not dangerous to bigger animals, but the coral snake is. Predators will not try to eat the coral snake because they are afraid of being bitten.

Ratsnake

Milksnake

King of snakes!

The longest snake in the world is the reticulated python, which grows up to 23 feet (7 m) metres long. It could wrap its body around a person 9 times!

Are frogs dangerous?

Some are! Even one lick of the poison arrow frog would make a predator very ill. Its brightly colored skin warns enemies that it is poisonous and dangerous to eat.

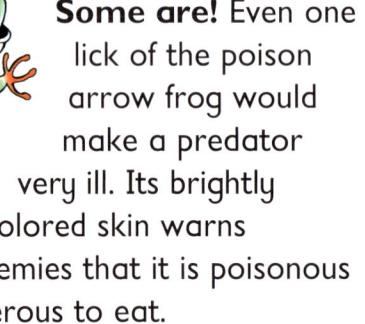

Can a lizard's tail fall off?

Some lizards have detachable tails! If a hungry hunter grabs the tail of a five-lined tree skink lizard, it will be left just holding a twitching tail. The lizard can quickly run away and will grow back a new tail.

Think

Can you remember how long it takes a snake to shed all of its skin?

Poison arrow frog

Why do snakes shed their skin?

A snake's skin does not grow with its body. This means that it has to shed its old skin as it grows bigger. It can take about two weeks for a snake to shed its skin completely.

Grass snake shedding skin

Ready to burst!

A snake has to swallow food whole as it can't chew. It opens its jaws extra wide to gulp down animals much larger than itself.

Which lizard can run on two legs?

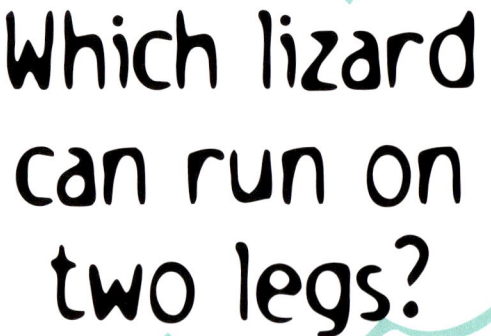

Fire-bellied toad

The crested water dragon from Asia can. In an emergency, this lizard can stand up on its back legs to run away from enemies. This is because it has large back feet and can run faster on two legs than on four over short distances.

Water dragon

Are toads colorful?

The fire-bellied toad has a bright red tummy. When it is threatened, the toad leaps away to safety, and the quick flash of red confuses its attacker and gives the frog more time to escape.

Sneaky hunters!

Crocodiles and alligators wait in shallow water for animals to come and drink, then they leap up and drag them under the water.

Play

How easy is it to sneak up on someone? See how quietly you can creep around the house without being noticed.

Do turtles play tricks?

The alligator snapper turtle looks like a rock as it lies on the ocean floor. The tip of its tongue looks like a juicy worm, which it waves at passing prey to tempt them into its jaws.

Do reptiles eat amphibians?

Some do. Most reptiles are meat eaters. The dwarf crocodile is so small that one frog is a big dinner. Frogs can jump very fast, but the dwarf crocodile snaps quickly at anything that makes a splash in the water near its jaws.

Dwarf crocodile

Glossary

amphibian (am-FIH-bee-un) An animal that spends the first part of its life in water and the rest on land.

basking (BASK-ing) To lie in the sun.

breeding grounds (BREED-ing GROWNDZ) Places where a certain kind of animal gives birth.

explorers (ek-SPLOR-erz) People who travel and look for new land.

hibernate (HY-bur-nayt) To spend the winter in a sleeplike state.

mate (MAYT) A partner for making babies.

prey (PRAY) An animal that is hunted by another animal for food.

reptile (REP-tyl) A cold-blooded animal with lungs and scales.

scales (SKAYLZ) A thin, dry piece of skin that forms the outer covering of snakes, lizards, and other reptiles.

tadpoles (TAD-pohlz) Baby frogs or toads that look like fish and live under the water.

Further Reading

Harris, Tim. *Amphibians*. Slimy, Scaly, Deadly Reptiles and Amphibians. New York: Gareth Stevens, 2010.

Rockwood, Leigh. *Tell Me the Difference Between an Alligator and a Crocodile. How Are They Different?* New York: PowerKids Press, 2013.

Royston, Angela. *Alligator: Killer King of the Swamp*. Top of the Food Chain. New York: Windmill Books, 2014.

Index

A
alligator, 21
amphibians, 5–11

C
caecilians, 5
chameleon, 12
crocodile(s), 4, 11, 21–22

E
egg(s), 8–11
enemies, 13, 18, 20
eyelids, 15

G
gecko(s), 12–13, 15

H
hibernate, 7
humans, 15

I
iguanas, 15

J
jaws, 19, 21–22

L
logs, 7

M
milksnake, 19
mouth, 11–12

N
newts, 5, 8

O
ocean, 21

P
pond(s), 6, 9
predator(s), 17–18
prey, 14, 16, 21

R
rattlesnakes, 14
reptile(s), 4, 10–11, 16, 22
rivers, 9
roads, 6

S
salamanders, 5
scales, 16
shell(s), 10–11
spawn, 8
stones, 7
stream(s), 6, 9

T
tadpoles, 8
towns, 6
tuatara, 4

W
worm, 21

Websites

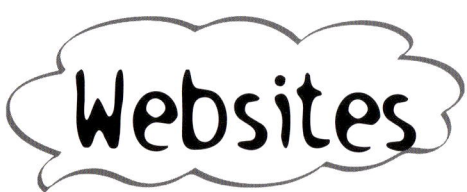

For web resources related to the subject of this book, go to:
www.windmillbooks.com/weblinks and select this book's title.